For Lily-Rose and her mum and dad – TB
To Mum and Dad – JC

First published in Great Britain in 2001 by Bloomsbury Publishing Plc
38 Soho Square, London, W1D 3HB
This paperback edition first published in 2002

Text copyright © Tony Bradman 2001
Illustrations copyright © Jason Cockroft 2001
The moral right of the author and illustrator has been asserted

A CIP catalogue record of this book is available from the British Library
ISBN 0 7475 5559 1

Printed in Hong Kong by Wing King Tong

1 3 5 7 9 10 8 6 4 2

DADDY'S LULLABY

Tony Bradman

illustrated by

Jason Cockcroft

BLOOMSBURY
CHILDREN'S
BOOKS

Hi there, pussy cat ... are you coming in with me?
Phew, it's been a long, long week. Am I glad it's Friday!

There you go ... I'll have some too.
And now I'm off to bed ... how about you?

Shhh ... Shhh ... tip-toe up the stairs ...
Everyone is fast asleep ...

But hey, what's this? Somebody's wide awake!
And not too happy, either …
There, there, little one, come to Daddy …
Let me chase that bad old dream away.

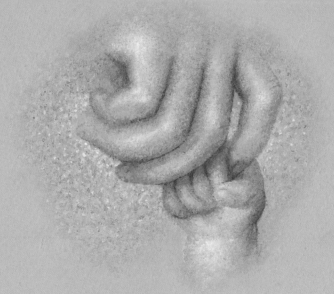

Hush now, everything's going to be all right.
Hush now, back to sleep …

No? too wide awake now?
Ok, let's go for a night-time stroll ...

But Shhh ... shhh ... don't make a peep!
Here's one big brother ...
It looks like he's had a good day!

And here's the best mother a baby could have …
You're a lucky baby, and I'm a lucky dad!

Still not tired? Well, we'd better go elsewhere ...
Shhh ... Shhh ... tip-toe down the stairs ...

Let's sit right here …
Now don't you cry … here's a little lullaby …

Rock-a-bye baby,
In Daddy's arms,
Daddy will hold you
Safe from all harm.

Daddy will love you
And work for our keep,
And rock you at night
When you can't sleep.

Rock-a-bye baby,
In Daddy's arms,
Daddy will hold you
Safe from all harm.

Daddy is with you,
So don't make a peep …
Rock-a-bye baby, Let's both … go … to …

... sleep!

Enjoy more great picture books from Bloomsbury …

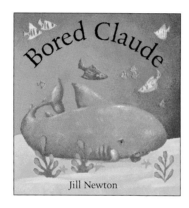

Bored Claude
Jill Newton

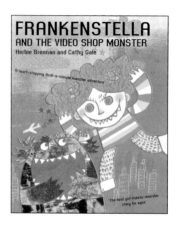

Frankenstella and the Video Shop Monster
Herbie Brennan & Cathy Gale

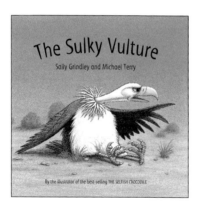

The Sulky Vulture
Sally Grindley & Michael Terry

Tickle Tickle
Dakari Hru & Ken Wilson-Max